JUNGLE SCRUMBLE

Written by

Kirstie Watson

Illustrated by

Tilia Rand-Bell

For my family.
Thank you for always believing in me.

Kirstie x

Telltale Tots Ltd.
www.telltaletots.co.uk

First published in the United Kingdom by Telltale Tots Publishing 2021

ISBN: 978-1-914937-03-3

A CIP catalogue record for this book is available from the British Library.

JUNGLE
SCRUMBLE

There are more than 100 butterflies in this book.
How many can you spot on each page?

Early one morning, the animals of the jungle were awoken by some awfully loud singing...

"Jungle scrumble for my tummy,
Jungle scrumble's very yummy.
But I just need a Jungle Mouse,
To come for dinner at my house!
Then I'll munch, slurp, gobble and burp.
Jungle scrumble, jungle scrumble!"

"It's PANTHER!" said Monkey.

"She's after Jungle Mouse again!

Come on, let's go and see what she's up to."

The animals crept closer, so they could listen in to Panther's plan...

"Yes! I'm going to make JUNGLE SCRUMBLE!

A delicious mix of my favourite things to eat!"

"And today I'll be adding a special ingredient... JUNGLE MOUSE.
But hmmm... how to catch her? WAIT, I've got it!

I'll invite her over to EAT. Genius!" she said with a chuckle.

Dearest Jungle Mouse

you are invited to join me for

dinner this evening.

I hope you can make it;

It wouldn't be the same

without you!

From

Panther

Then she posted the invitation, feeling very pleased with herself.

"Hmmm," said Elephant, "I think it's time we put an end to Panther's dinner plans. Our friend Jungle Mouse is going to be OFF the menu!" The other animals agreed, and together they began to hatch their own plan.

WHISPER
WHISPER
WHISPER

Once the plan was decided,

Monkey went in first...

"Hello, Panther! What are you up to?" she asked.

"Oh! Hi, Monkey!" said Panther. "I've invited

Jungle Mouse over to EAT ... I mean, to eat TOGETHER.

So, I'm making jungle scrumble..."

"Lovely," Monkey said quickly, "you should add some nice, rubbery BANANA SKINS!"

"Errr... Well, NO, I don't like..." but before Panther could stop her, Monkey tossed in some banana skins, then swung off into the trees.

Panther did **NOT** like banana skins, but they were soon forgotten as she returned to her dinner plans...

"Jungle scrumble for my tummy,
Jungle scrumble's very yummy.
But I just need a Jungle Mouse,
To come for dinner at my house!
Then I'll munch, slurp, gobble and burp.
Jungle scrumble, jungle scrumble!"

Elephant went in next.

"Hi, Panther! What are you doing?" he asked.

"I'm having Jungle Mouse for dinner... sorry, I mean, Jungle Mouse is COMING over for DINNER. So, I'm making jungle scrumble, it's....."

"Lovely! Why not add some nice LEAVES? It's important to eat plenty of green things, isn't it?" said Elephant

before Panther could finish.

"I... don't think..." But before Panther could stop him, Elephant sprinkled in some leaves.

"Enjoy your dinner!" said Elephant.

Panther didn't like leaves, but it was too late now,
so she just stirred them in.

"Jungle scrumble for my tummy,

Jungle scrumble's very yummy.

But I just need a Jungle Mouse,

To come for dinner at my house!

Then I'll munch, slurp, gobble and burp.

Jungle scrumble, jungle scrumble!"

Hippo was up next.

"Wow, Panther! What's going on here?" he asked.

"I'm going to EAT Jungle Mouse... sorry...

I'm going to eat WITH Jungle Mouse.

So, I'm making jungle scrumble! It's..."

Panther started to explain.

" Great! You should put in some MUD!" Hippo suggested. "It'll add a nice, earthy taste!"

Panther wasn't sure about the mud, but it was too late.

Hippo had already sploshed some into the pot.

"It's going to be PERFECT!

just wait and see!" said Hippo.

"Oh YES, it is!" agreed Panther, forgetting all about the mud. "Ha ha! Those animals have NO idea what I'm planning for their friend!"

"Jungle scrumble for my tummy,

Jungle scrumble's very yummy.

But I just need a Jungle Mouse,

To come for dinner at my house!

Then I'll munch, slurp, gobble and burp.

Jungle scrumble, jungle scrumble!"

Last up was Jungle Mouse.

"Hello, Panther! I'm ready to EAT!" she said.

"Not quite!" whispered Panther.

"Pardon?" said Jungle Mouse.

"Oh, nothing." Panther grinned.

"I'm glad you're here, you're just in time.

Come and help me stir the pot...

it's almost ready... it just needs

one... more... thing..."

Suddenly, the other animals appeared.

"Oh. What are YOU doing here?" asked Panther.

"You weren't invited!"

"Your scrumble looks DELICIOUS!" said elephant. "Have you tried it yet, Panther?"

"Well, no, I was um... waiting for Jungle mouse," Panther replied.

"NONSENSE! Try some!" Monkey insisted, spooning some into Panther's mouth.

Panther GULPED.

The banana skins were horribly RUBBERY.

The green leaves were terribly BITTER.

The mud was awfully SLOPPY.

And all together it tasted...

"YUUUUUUCK!"

Panther was utterly horrified by the DISGUSTING mixture. She SPAT and SPLUTTERED and ran off into the night.

"That will teach Panther a lesson she'll NEVER forget!" said Monkey.

Their plan had worked - Jungle Mouse was now officially OFF the menu!

And so the animals danced and sang together in celebration...

"Jungle scrumble's very yucky,

Jungle Mouse is very lucky.

Together we have saved the day,

And Panther's gone and ran away.

Yucky, chewy, crunchy, spewy!

Jungle scrumble, Jungle scrumble."

JUNGLES OF THE WORLD

A jungle is land covered with dense forest and vegetation, usually in warm places where it rains a lot. They are found in Central America, northern South America, West Africa, and Southeast Asia (see the green areas of the map). It is thought that more than half of the animal species in the world live in jungles and rainforests. They are also home to an estimated 40,000 species of plants.

THE REAL ANIMALS OF THE JUNGLE

Panthers are good tree climbers and often hunt and live in trees. They are carnivores (and don't eat Jungle Scrumble in real life). They are nocturnal, preferring to hunt at night and rest during the day. The panther can run up to 71 mph [114 kph] (that's as fast as a car travelling on the motorway!).

There are many species of rodent that live in the jungle – including jungle mice. Mice tend to be nocturnal, and come out at night. They are omnivorous and eat a variety of food depending on what is available, including: insects, seeds, fruits, flowers and nuts.

Monkeys live in the jungles of Africa, Central America, South America and Asia. They live mostly in trees (with the exception of baboons). Most monkeys are herbivores and eat fruits, leaves and nuts. Some of the more common jungle monkeys include: chimpanzees, howler monkeys, marmosets, spider monkeys and capuchins.

Jungle, or Forest, elephants are a smaller subspecies of African elephants and inhabit the jungles and rainforests of West and Central Africa. They can grow up to 3 metres high and weigh up to 5 tonnes. Forest elephants are herbivores and live on a diet of foraged leaves, seeds, fruit and tree bark. They tend to live together in family groups.

The common hippopotamus (Hippo) live in sub-Saharan Africa. They spend their days swimming, walking, wallowing in mud and wading in calm rivers and lakes to keep cool. At night, they roam the land for their favourite thing to eat: grass.

Thank you for buying this book!

I hope you've enjoyed meeting the jungle scrumble gang!?

Did you know that reader reviews are like

MAGIC for an author like me?

They help bring attention to the book, and help

others decide if they'd like to buy it too.

So, if you like this book, please consider...

1. Telling your FRIENDS.

2. Telling ME! I'd love to hear from you.

Send me a message via: kirstiewatsonauthor.co.uk

3. Leaving a REVIEW on Amazon or Goodreads.

Kirstie x

Get a free activity pack!

Download from: kirstiewatsonauthor.co.uk/resources

Find out more about Kirstie and her books:

facebook.com/kirstiewatsonauthor

instagram.com/kirstie_watson_author

Printed in Great Britain
by Amazon